P9-EDO-141

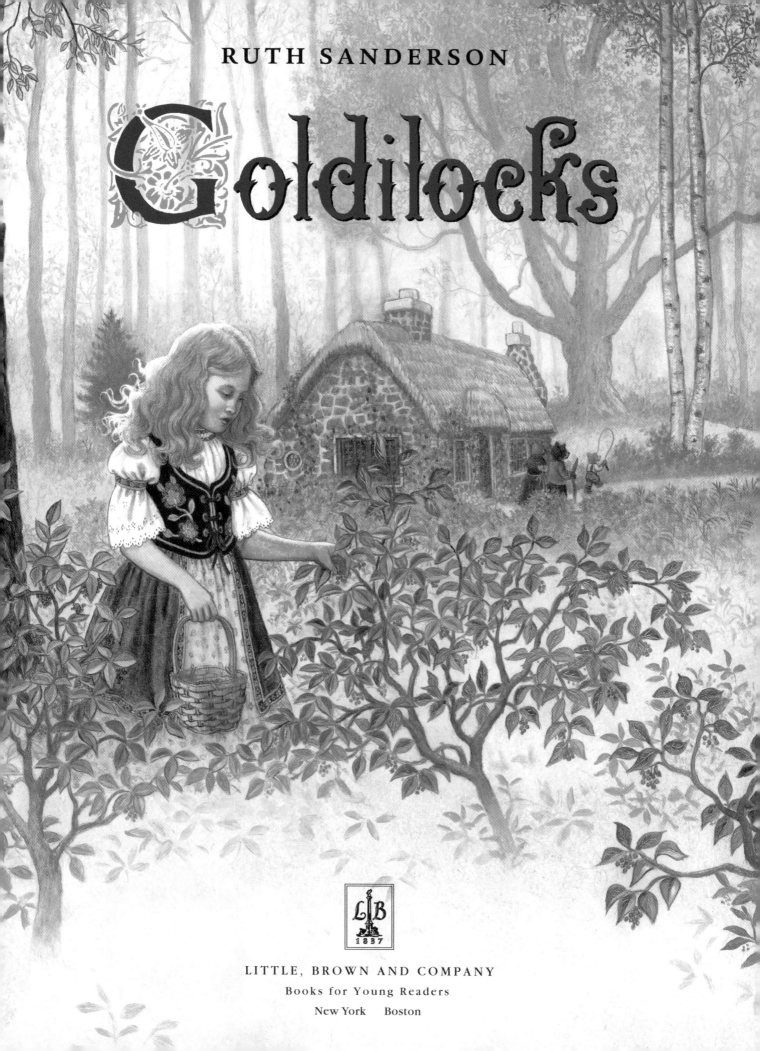

RUTH SANDERSON

Goldilocks

LITTLE, BROWN AND COMPANY

Books for Young Readers

New York   Boston

Little, Brown Books for Young Readers

Hachette Book Group • 237 Park Avenue, New York, NY 10017
Visit our Web site at www.lb-kids.com

Little, Brown Books for Young Readers is a division of Hachette Book Group, Inc.
The Little, Brown name and logo are trademarks of Hachette Book Group, Inc.

First Edition: October 2009

Library of Congress Cataloging-in-Publication Data

Sanderson, Ruth.
  Goldilocks / retold and illustrated by Ruth Sanderson.—1st ed.
    p. cm.
  Summary: After finding the bears' cottage in the woods and making a
mess inside, Goldilocks helps the family clean up and enjoys a nice meal.
  ISBN 978-0-316-77885-5
  [1. Folklore. 2. Bears—Folklore.] I. Goldilocks and the three bears.
English. II. Title.
  PZ8.1.S235Gol 2009
  398.22—dc22
  [E]
                                        2008045298

10 9 8 7 6 5 4 3 2 1 QUAL Printed in China

The artwork for this book was created with graphite pencil on Bristol drawing paper
and painted with Old Holland oils. The text was set in Legacy.

Once upon a time, there were three bears that lived in a little stone cottage deep in the woods: a great big Papa Bear, a middle-sized Momma Bear, and a wee little Baby Bear. Every morning, the bears took a walk while their porridge was cooling off.

One day, while the bears were still on their walk, a visitor arrived at their house. Her name was Goldilocks.

Goldilocks loved to pick blueberries. That morning, she wandered from bush to bush to bush, and before she knew it, she was standing in front of a cottage she had never seen before.

She wondered who lived there and knocked on the door. When no one answered, Goldilocks forgot her manners and walked right in!

Goldilocks smelled the bears' porridge and rushed over to the table.
She was very hungry.

First she tasted the porridge in the great big bowl, but it was too hot.

Then she tasted the porridge in the middle-sized bowl, but it was too cold.

Finally, she tasted the porridge in the wee little bowl, and it was just right.
Goldilocks ate it all up, every bite.

Across the room, Goldilocks saw three chairs in front of a cozy fireplace. First she tried to sit on the biggest chair, but it was too high.

Then she tried the middle-sized chair, but it was too wide.

Finally, she sat in the wee little chair and it was just right. But Goldilocks rocked so hard in the chair that it broke into pieces!

Goldilocks began to feel tired after all of her adventures.
She peered through a doorway and saw three beds.

First she climbed into the biggest bed, but it was too hard.

Then she climbed into the middle-sized bed, but it was too soft.

Finally, she climbed into the wee little bed, and it was just right.
Goldilocks pulled the quilt up to her chin and fell fast asleep.

When the three bears returned home and found their front door wide open, they ran inside.

"Someone's been tasting my porridge!" said Papa Bear in his great big voice.

"Someone's been tasting *my* porridge!" said Momma Bear in her middle-sized voice.

"Someone's been tasting my porridge!" said Baby Bear in his wee little voice. "And it's all tasted away!"

The three bears discovered a mess across the room.

"Someone's been sitting in my chair!" said Papa Bear in his great big voice.

"Someone's been sitting in *my* chair!" said Momma Bear in her middle-sized voice.

"Someone's been sitting in my chair," said Baby Bear in his wee little voice.
"And it's broken all to pieces!"

The three bears peeked into the bedroom to see what else they'd find.

"Someone's been sleeping in my bed!" said Papa Bear with a great big growl.

"Someone's been sleeping in *my* bed!" said Momma Bear
with a middle-sized growl.

"Someone's been sleeping in my bed!"
said Baby Bear with a wee little growl.
"And there she is!"

At the sound of Baby Bear's shrill voice, Goldilocks woke up with a start. She was so afraid she could not speak.

"Can I keep her?" asked Baby Bear.

"No, dear," said Momma Bear, "but you can keep an eye on her while she makes up the beds."

Baby Bear played with his blocks while Goldilocks straightened up the quilts. Then she followed Baby Bear to the other room, where Momma Bear was weaving a new seat for his chair.

"May I help?" asked Goldilocks.

Momma Bear smiled at Goldilocks, handed her some canes, and showed her how to weave them in and out.

Papa Bear made new legs for the chair and soon it was as good as new.
But Baby Bear was not happy.

"Momma," said Baby Bear in his wee little voice, "I'm hungry."

"I'm hungry, too," said Momma Bear in her middle-sized voice.

"I'm very, very hungry," said Papa Bear in his great big voice.

Goldilocks backed away from the three bears. Were they going to eat *her* for breakfast? Then she saw her basket near the door, and Goldilocks had an idea.

"Blueberries are very good for breakfast," said Goldilocks.

"Blueberries are tasty!" said Baby Bear in his wee little voice.

"But I know something even tastier!" said Momma Bear in her middle-sized voice.

"And we have all the ingredients!" said Papa Bear in his great big voice. He smiled a great big toothy bear smile. Momma Bear smiled at Goldilocks, too. And Baby Bear smiled a wee little bear smile.

"Oh, boy . . ." said Baby Bear.

"Blueberry muffins!" he cheered. Baby Bear brought a jar of honey to the table. Papa Bear poured the blueberries into a bowl. Momma Bear took out flour, baking soda, salt, milk, butter, and eggs.

Papa Bear stirred the ingredients together, spooned the batter into a
muffin tin, and popped it into the oven. Momma Bear put the kettle on.
Goldilocks helped Baby Bear set the table.

And they all had tea. And blueberry muffins, warm from the oven.

Papa Bear's Blueberry Muffins

- 2 cups flour
- ¼ teaspoon salt
- 3 teaspoons baking powder
- ½ teaspoon cinnamon
- 1 cup milk
- 4 tablespoons honey
- 4 tablespoons sugar
- ½ stick melted butter
- 1 beaten egg
- 1 cup blueberries

Preheat oven to 400 degrees. Mix together flour with salt, sugar, baking powder, and cinnamon. In a separate bowl, combine milk, honey, butter, and egg. Add to dry ingredients and stir to moisten. Add blueberries. Fill greased muffin tin ⅔ full and bake 20-25 minutes until golden brown. Makes 12 muffins. Yum!